This book belongs to:

_____

_____

For Team McCallum:
Ben, Toby, Ella and Charlie.

Mantra Lingua
Global House
303 Ballards Lane
London, N12 8NP
www.mantralingua.com

Touch the arrow with the RecorderPEN to start

⇒ □ ○ ○
Start Info English Language

Paresseux lentement regardait de sa branche. Il ne bougeait pas beaucoup.

Sloth slowly watched from his branch. He didn't move very much.

Singe se balança près de lui. « Regarde-moi, Paresseux ! Essaie de m'attraper ! »

Monkey swung past.
"Look at me, Sloth! Try and catch me!"

Paresseux regarda Singe
disparaître dans les arbres…

…et soupira.

Sloth watched Monkey
disappear into the trees…

…and sighed.

Il regarda les lémurs sauter,
les panthères s'élancer
et les orangs-outangs *jongler*.

He watched lemurs leap,
panthers pounce
and orangutans do *the jungle juggle.*

Et Paresseux lentement…
lentement…
lentement ferma les yeux.

And Sloth slowly…
slowly…
slowly closed his eyes.

« Tu ne peux pas m'attraper, Paresseux ! » rit Singe.

"You can't catch me, Sloth!" Monkey laughed.

Paresseux regarda Singe virevolter sur les branches, se balancer jusqu'aux équipes sélectionnées… *et soupira.*

Sloth watched Monkey spin about on the branches, swinging off to the team selections…

…and sighed.

Chacal se contentait de regarder pendant que chaque créature faisait de son mieux.
Il choisit Singe en premier parce que Singe gagnait *toujours*.

Jackal looked on as every creature tried their best.
She chose Monkey first as Monkey *always* won.

Personne ne choisit Paresseux. Il n'y avait pas de course pour traîner.

Nobody chose Sloth.
There was no race for
hanging about.

L'équipe travaillait dur. Ils
voulaient tous vraiment gagner
les jeux de la jungle.

The team
worked hard.
They all really
wanted to win
the jungle
games.

« Je vais gagner ! » cria Singe. « Personne ne peut m'attraper ! »
Tous les animaux regardèrent Singe... et soupirèrent.

"I'm going to win!" called Monkey.
"No one can catch me!"
All the animals watched Monkey... and sighed.

Après une longue nuit agitée, le soleil finalement apparut. Et avec lui sont arrivées les équipes compétitives.

La jungle était vivante de sport.

After a long, restless night the sun finally appeared. And along with it came the competing teams.

The jungle was alive with sport.

Lentement, Paresseux changea
de branche pour regarder les tigres
culbuter, les toucans danser, les
éléphants barrir et les grenouilles
sautiller,
bondir   et sauter !

Slowly, Sloth moved branch to watch the tigers tumble,
the toucans tango, the elephants humph and the
frogs hop,
skip
and jump!

Bientôt, il ne restait plus qu'une seule course.
« Cela va être fastoche » dit Singe alors qu'il se préparait.
« Je suis aussi rapide que le vent. Personne, *je veux dire personne*, ne peut m'attraper ! »

Soon there was only one race left.
"It'll be a breeze," said Monkey as he got ready.
"I'm as fast as the wind. No one, *I mean no one*, can catch me!"

Singe se lança des rameaux
aux branches et des branches
aux plantes grimpantes, se
balançant de plus en plus vite.
Tout le monde acclamait
alors que Singe gagnait du terrain.

Monkey raced from bough to branch to vine,
swinging faster and faster.
Everyone cheered as the gap got wider.

Singe sauta et attrapa la plus haute
branche de l'arbre…

Monkey leapt and grabbed the
highest branch of the tree…

Paresseux lentement… lentement…
se leva sur sa branche.

Sloth slowly…
slowly…
stood up on his branch.

Il allongea ses longs bras,
puis…

ZOOM !

He stretched his long arms,
then…

WHOOSH!

Tout le monde acclama alors que Paresseux *finalement* rattrapait Singe !

Everyone cheered as Sloth *finally* caught Monkey!

JUNGLE FACTS

Sloths are surprisingly
good at swimming!

Lemurs use their big tails to signal to each other.

Panthers are really good at climbing trees.

When a male and female toucan like each other,
they use their beaks to throw fruit to each other.

Elephants make lots of interesting noises.
They grunt, purr, bellow, whistle and trumpet.

Monkeys live in groups called troops.

A tiger's roar can be heard more than a mile away.

If people don't stop chopping down the jungle,
very soon there won't be any jungle left.